BUBBLEMANIA

For Adam, who made it possible
S.D.

For Samantha, my #1 fan
B.B.

BUBBLEMANIA

Written by
Sheila Dalton

Illustrated by
Bob Beeson

Orca Book Publishers

Victoria, B.C.

Once there was a little boy named David who loved to make bubbles.
He made big ones and small ones, long ones and tall ones.
One day he made a very, very big bubble.
Wow, he thought, that must be the most giant bubble in the whole world.

That giant bubble flew up. That giant bubble sank down.
And when it hit the ground it bounced. It bounced once.
It bounced twice. It landed on the baby next door.

It picked her up!

Now inside that bubble was:

1 baby clapping

The bubble got bigger. It blew into two sparrows.
It bent and stre-e-e-e-tched and went

GA-LUMF.

Now inside that
bubble were:

1 baby clapping

2 sparrows flapping

The bubble got even bigger. It bounced onto three
monarch butterflies resting in a tree...

BOINGG, BOINGG, BOINGG!

Now inside that bubble were:

1 baby clapping

2 sparrows flapping

3 monarch butterflies

The bubble bounced onto four dogs lounging around a
fire hydrant. It gulped up them up.

Those dogs were really surprised.

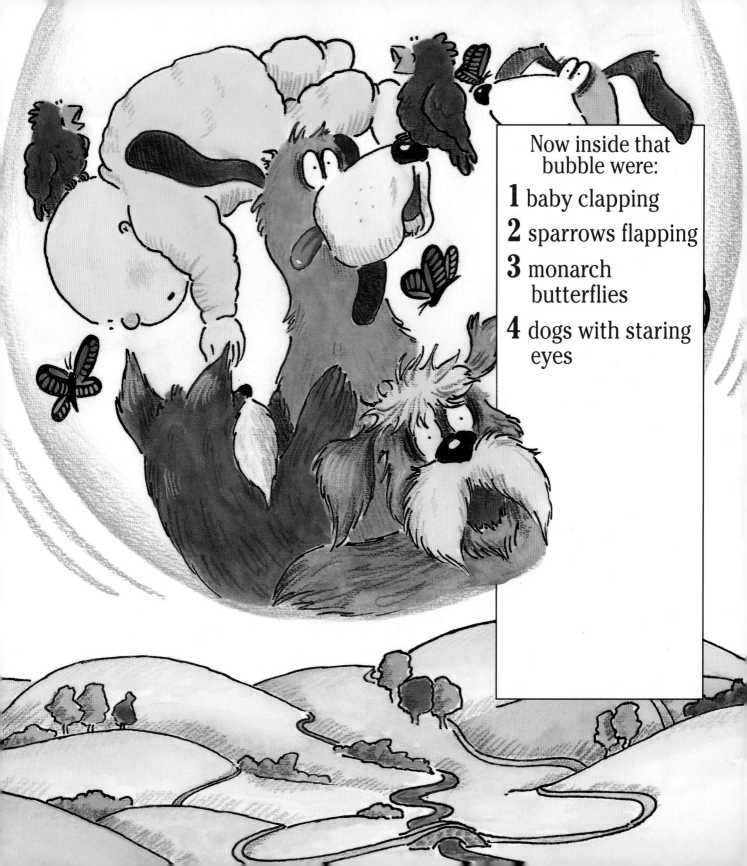

Now inside that bubble were:

1 baby clapping

2 sparrows flapping

3 monarch butterflies

4 dogs with staring eyes

The bubble blew into five cats sitting on a fence.

It gobbled them up.

Now inside that bubble were:

1 baby clapping

2 sparrows flapping

3 monarch butterflies

4 dogs with staring eyes

5 cats with lashing tails

The bubble got bigger. It bounced right onto a table
at a garage sale.

It ga-lumfed up six toys.

Now inside that bubble were:

1 baby clapping

2 sparrows flapping

3 monarch butterflies

4 dogs with staring eyes

5 cats with lashing tails

6 toys that were for sale

The bubble bounced along until it came to the annual mouse race.

BOINGG, BOINGG, BOINGG, BOINGG, BOINGG, BOINGG, BOINGG!!

Now inside that bubble were:

1 baby clapping
2 sparrows flapping
3 monarch butterflies
4 dogs with staring eyes
5 cats with lashing tails
6 toys that were for sale
7 mice in trucks

PET SHOW
TODAY

The bubble went bouncing out over the park and landed
on a whole bunch of ducks.

QUACK, QUACK, QUACK, QUACK! What a racket!

Now inside that bubble were:

1 baby clapping

2 sparrows flapping

3 monarch butterflies

4 dogs with staring eyes

5 cats with lashing tails

6 toys that were for sale

7 mice in trucks

8 quacking ducks

The bubble got S-O-O-O-O BIG it began to look like
a flying elephant. It went WIBBLE-WOBBLE, GA-BOING, GA-BOING
down the main street of the town.

Then it bounced onto the heads of nine people wearing sunhats.
Uh-oh!

Now inside that bubble were:

1 baby clapping

2 sparrows flapping

3 monarch butterflies

4 dogs with staring eyes

5 cats with lashing tails

6 toys that were for sale

7 mice in trucks

8 quacking ducks

9 hats it didn't own

The bubble went WIBBLE-WOBBLE, BIBBLE-BOBBLE, GA-BOING, GA-BOING — into the middle of a bunch of clowns eating ice-cream.

Guess what happened?

Now inside that bubble were:

1 baby clapping
2 sparrows flapping
3 monarch butterflies
4 dogs with staring eyes
5 cats with lashing tails
6 toys that were for sale
7 mice in trucks
8 quacking ducks
9 hats it didn't own
10 melting ice-cream cones

PARADE STARTS HERE TODAY

And David was thinking, enough is enough!
When that giant bubble WIBBLED and WOBBLED,
BIBBLED and BOBBLED, JIGGLED and WIGGLED,
and GA-BONGED all the way to the great big field behind
the town hall, David knew what he was going to do.

The bubble sank down low. David took a safety pin out of his pants. His pants fell down. He pulled them back up. Then he aimed the pin. He pricked that bubble hard. "Happy landings!" he yelled.

You can imagine what happened then–

The hats, the baby, cones and toys,
the dogs all making lots of noise,
birds and cats and mice in trucks,
butterflies and quacking ducks, came
rolling, falling, tumbling down,
upon the grass behind the town...

and on David!

David's Giant Bubble Mix

1/2 cup Joy dishwashing detergent
5 cups clean, cold water
stir slowly until completely blended, skimming off any
froth or small bubbles on the surface. A smooth mixture
without surface froth is the secret to really big bubbles.

To make your own bubble wands:
Thread about 30" of string through two straws and
tie in a knot.
(figure 1)
Get an adult to help you twist coathangers into
different shapes.
(figures 2 & 3)

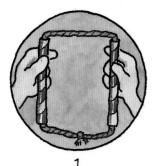

1.

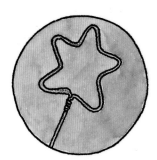

2.   3.

Publication assistance provided by The Canada Council.

Orca Book Publishers
PO Box 5626 Stn. B
Victoria, B.C. Canada
V8R 6S4

Design by Bob Beeson and Christine Toller
Printed in Hong Kong

Canadian Cataloguing in Publication Data

Dalton, Sheila,
Bubblemania

ISBN 0–920501–75–3

1. Counting — Juvenile literature.   I. Beeson, Bob, 1950–   II. Title.
QA113.D34 1992   j513.2'11   C92–091107–2